J.P. and the GIANT OCTOPUS

ANA CRESPO

Pictures by
ERICA SIROTICH

Albert Whitman & Company
Chicago, Illinois

To JP and Duda.
Thank you for being an infinite source of inspiration.
Love you!—AC

For Nick,
who showed me the way—ES

Library of Congress Cataloging-in-Publication
data is on file with the publisher.

Text copyright © 2015 by Ana Crespo
Pictures copyright © 2015 by Albert Whitman & Company
Pictures by Erica Sirotich
Published in 2015 by Albert Whitman & Company
ISBN 978-0-8075-3975-0

Printed in China
10 9 8 7 6 5 4 3 2 1 HH 20 19 18 17 16 15

Design by Jordan Kost

For more information about Albert Whitman & Company,
visit our web site at www.albertwhitman.com.

I am JP the shark.

I am fast. I am strong.

I am brave.

But sometimes I don't feel like a brave shark.

Sometimes I feel afraid.

Like when I met the giant octopus.

The giant octopus tried to cover our car with slime.

ONE WAY

Then it tried to smash us.

I couldn't see anything.
And there were creepy noises all around.

I almost cried.
I was so scared.

Then I remembered I am a brave shark.

I showed my big shark teeth.

I did a sharky dance.

I made some
sharky sounds.

The giant octopus was afraid of me!

It cried.

I felt sorry. I apologized.

The giant octopus just wanted to play.

See you next time,
giant octopus.

I am JP.

I am fast. I am strong.

Sometimes I feel afraid...

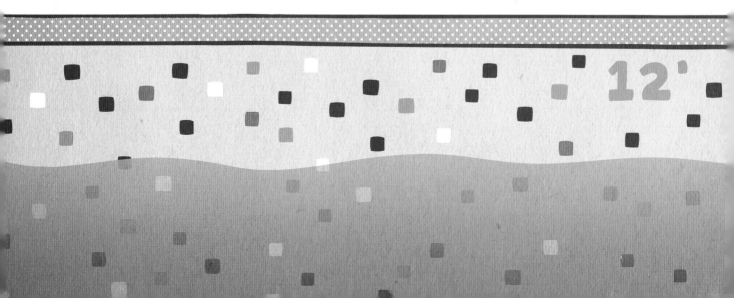

but I know that
I am brave!

A Note to Parents and Teachers from the Author

Feeling afraid or fearful is a natural response to unfamiliar situations. Fear makes us cautious and alert to possible dangers. But when fear is too intense, it can become an obstacle to living a healthy life. Children can be fearful because they are still unfamiliar with most of the world surrounding them.

JP and the Giant Octopus was the first book I wrote in the JP series and it is based on a real-life experience with my son. The real JP was about three years old when he went to a car wash for the first time. He was very scared. I remember my daughter, who was ten, hugging JP while I held his hands. I assured him that the car wash "monster" was good and that it was helping us clean our car. He calmed down, and after that experience, visiting the car wash became a fun activity.

Many parents and caregivers have experienced similar situations when their child is nearly paralyzed with fear. On the other hand, some children can be fearless because they don't recognize danger. The temperament of each child will play a role in his tendency to feel fear. In addition, a child's vivid imagination, like JP's, can increase his fear or, if given the right coaching, help him have fun.

Here are some ways to help your child work through his or her fears:

Caregivers should **acknowledge the child's fear**, even if the fear seems unreasonable. And they should **never make fun of the fear**. When a child is old enough to express her feelings, even if not perfectly well, **listen**. Understanding what scares the child will help you assist her in coping with her fear. **Clarify false impressions** the child has of her surroundings. You can do this with fun activities such as reading or role-playing, just as JP does with the car wash, to help explain why she doesn't need to be afraid. Some fears are rational, like a fear of bees, for example, so the goal is to **maintain a balance.** A child's fear of bees should not overwhelm her but keep her alert to avoid harm.

Always **stay calm.** Your own fears or anxiety when dealing with your child's problem may make the situation worse. **Reassure** the child that you're there to support her. Give the child an opportunity to **self soothe**. Knowing how to handle stress and anxiety is a useful skill. In the story, JP has the support of his doggy sidekick. However, JP is the one who puts on his mask and deals with his fear in a way that feels appropriate for him. Lastly, **encourage your child to experiment**, from trying different foods, to new games, to playing with new kids. The more experience a child has, the more comfortable she will feel in unfamiliar situations, and the better she will know how to handle them.

If you feel your child is extremely fearful, or if you need help dealing with her (or your own) feelings, talk to your doctor. Extreme anxiety or fears that interfere with the child's everyday life may need extra attention.

Please note that I am not a specialist in the field of children's emotions. My experience and knowledge come from being a parent and conducting my own research. For additional information specific to your needs, please seek a professional opinion.

References:

Honig, Alice Sterling, Susan A. Miller, and Ellen Booth Church. "Ages & stages: What makes children anxious." *Scholastic.* 2015. http://www.scholastic.com/teachers/article/ages-stages-what-makes-children-anxious.

Poulsen, Alison. "Fearful Children." *So what I really meant.* 2015. http://www.sowhatireallymeant.com/articles/parenting/fearful-children.

State Government of Victoria and La Trobe University. "Fear and anxiety—children." *Better Health Channel.* February 9, 2015. http://www.betterhealth.vic.gov.au/bhcv2/bhcarticles.nsf/pages/Fear_and_anxiety_children.